DRAGON CHILD

The Pearl Quest

GILL VICKERY

Illustrated by
MIKE LOVE

A & C BLACK
AN IMPRINT OF BLOOMSBURY
LONDON NEW DELHI NEW YORK SYDNEY

- ■ Major Towns
- ● Villages
- ⊹ Ports
- ✪ Dragon Keeps
- ★ Dragon Haven

Western Sea

Volcanic Keeps

West Eldkeiler Mts

Stoplar

Hamar

Iserborg

Sanderhof

DRAGON CHILD

To Elizabeth, my DragonDaughter.

With many thanks to David Wheeler, the Swan Herd of
Abbotsbury Swannery, for his invaluable help and advice.
Any swan-related errors are entirely the author's own.

First published 2014 by A & C Black,
an imprint of Bloomsbury Publishing Plc
50 Bedford Square
London WC1B 3DP

www.bloomsbury.com
Bloomsbury is a trademark of Bloomsbury Publishing Plc

ISBN 978-1-4729-0450-8

A CIP catalogue for this book is available from the British Library.

Printed and Bound by CPI Group (UK) Ltd, Croydon CR0 4YY

1 3 5 7 9 10 8 6 4 2

MIX
Paper from
responsible sources
FSC® C020471
www.fsc.org

The Story So Far...

The six High Witch sisters of Tulay stole the DragonQueen's jewels of power. In revenge, a dragon kidnapped the youngest witch's child, a girl called Tia. Raised by the dragons and tormented for being a witch-brat, Tia set out to steal back the jewels to prove herself a true DragonChild. She is helped in the quest by her DragonBrother, Finn, who has the gift of being able to blend invisibly into any background, and a jackdaw called Loki.

Tia has recovered five jewels: the emerald, which grants the power to talk to animals, the opal, which lets its owner change shape, the topaz, which controls the weather, the sapphire which can transport the holder anywhere in the blink of an eye and the ruby which stops time. Finn safeguards the jewels, except for the emerald which Tia keeps with her so that she can talk to Loki.

Now there is just one jewel left to steal: the pearl which heals and mends. But this gem is in the power of Tia's own mother, the High Witch Ondine, who knows that the thief is coming for her pearl. Tia is in greater danger than at any time in her quest.

Chapter One

The Shadow Snake

The spell against dragons wrapped itself like a great shadowy snake round the lands of Holmurholt. It whipped along the hills encircling the plain and the rivers below. The ghostly serpent's head darted restlessly here and there, its eyes flickering, its tongue dabbing in and out. Tia shivered.

Her DragonBrother, Finn, was looking down on Tulay's five sparkling rivers flowing into a huge blue lake set in the middle of the plain. Dozens of small islands, crowded with buildings, dotted the water.

'I'd love a swim,' the little dragon said wistfully.

Tia rounded fiercely on her DragonBrother. 'You mustn't even think of trying.' Finn couldn't see the spell and had no idea how powerful it was.

'I could disguise myself. I've been in all the other lands and towns and never come to any harm.'

'This is different,' Tia insisted. 'The High Witch must know that all the other jewels have been stolen and she'll be protecting the pearl with her most powerful magic. The spell against dragons will be even stronger than the one that caught me in Stoplar when I changed into a dragon.'

Loki the jackdaw was perching on the dragon's shoulder. 'Does Finn want to go into Holmurholt?' he asked Tia.

She nodded. 'But I'm sure the High Witch has made the spell stronger than ever.'

Loki hopped onto the grass. 'I'll try and keep him from going into Holmurholt, though it's hard when I can't speak to him.'

Tia told Finn what the jackdaw had said to her. The little dragon puffed out a cloud of hot smoke over both of them. Loki squawked in protest and flew up into a tree.

'I think you should give me the emerald to look after,' Finn said to Tia.

'Why?' Tia said, surprised. 'I know the other jewels are too strong for me to use but the emerald is safe.'

'High Witch Hyldi almost snatched it from you when you were fighting her in Askarlend. This High Witch might do the same. She'd find a way to use it to work evil magic.'

8

That was true. All the same, Tia didn't want to surrender the emerald. 'How will I talk to Loki?'

'You won't be able to.' Finn said. This time he blew sweet-smelling smoke gently over Tia. 'You'll have to give up the emerald soon anyway and give it back to the DragonQueen.'

Tia knew Finn was right. She unfastened the chain round her neck and slipped off the emerald ring she'd kept for so long. It lay in her palm, glinting in dozens of shades from the deep green of the ocean depths to the pale jade of a newly unfurled leaf.

Reluctantly she thrust the ring at Finn. Now her chain only carried the locket with pictures of her lost parents in it.

Finn delicately unpicked the emerald's gold setting with his claws and freed the jewel. He tossed the ring away. 'Put the emerald in the pouch.'

Tia opened the pouch Finn wore round his neck and dropped the emerald inside where it lay with the opal, the topaz, the sapphire and the ruby.

'You'd better leave your locket as well,' Finn said. 'She...you know, the High Witch...' He meant Tia's mother. 'She might recognise it. She'd want to know how you got hold of it.'

Tia opened the locket. She'd covered the picture of her mother but she took a last look at the portrait of her beloved father before she snapped it shut. She dropped the chain and locket into the pouch. 'It feels strange without them.'

Finn butted her shoulder gently with his nose. 'Will you be all right when you see her?'

'Yes. She stole the pearl and I'm going to get it back. I don't care about anything else.'

Tia hugged Finn's muzzle, picked up her bag and walked down the hill towards Holmurholt.

Tia made good progress down the grassy hillsides and past clumps of beech trees until she came to the snake spell. Even though it only attacked dragons Tia paused when she saw its ugly head and huge fangs close to.

She waited for the head to slither past as the spell snake hurtled on its way around the border of Holmurholt.

'Now!' Tia told herself and plunged into the spell. It was hard to see inside the shadowy snake, and she stumbled and fell. Before she could scramble to her feet the snake was back, its gaping mouth heading straight for her. Tia closed her eyes as the gigantic jaws engulfed her.

It can't hurt me, she thought and threw herself down the hill. She rolled over, faster and faster, until she crashed into a tree and all the breath was knocked out of her in a whoosh.

She lay for a while getting her breath back, then opened her eyes. The blue sky of early summer arced over her and beech leaves rustled in a breeze. She sat up. Above her the snake spell squirmed along the hilltops.

'I'm glad that's over,' she said.

She got to her feet and walked on towards the plain.

Chapter Two

The Swans of Holmurholt

Swathes of reeds, lush green fields and groves of trees grew between the five rivers. Boats, large and small, plied up and down. When they reached the central lake they passed under bridges linking the small islands. Tall, stately buildings crowded the centre of each island, leaving a fringe of grass and reeds at their edges.

Tia crossed from island to island, weaving through bustling streets, past houses, inns, workplaces and shops. She stopped and peered curiously into a shop selling feather goods. Plumes like cascades of white water sprang from hats and helmets. Snowy feathers trimmed the edges of garments. There was even a cloak made entirely of black and white plumage.

There were smaller things too: long feathery scarves, fans and quill pens.

Tia walked on until she was close to the centre of the lake where the largest island was. To her surprise, the palace there wasn't as spectacular as those of the other High Witches. It was more like an imposing and elegant house. The small clusters of dwellings around it were also modest. They were built of wood with thatched or grass roofs. Most had pens with goats or pigs, and hens.

But what surprised Tia most were the hundreds of swans floating on the broad stretch of lake that surrounded the island, cutting it off from the others. Even more swans were grazing on the grassy margins of the large island and the ones nearest to it. Others were foraging in rivulets and pools or sitting on reedy nests. It was late spring. The swans' eggs would soon hatch.

'Help!'

Tia swung round. A nesting swan was puffing herself up and beating her wings at a fox. It darted to one side. The swan hissed, neck snaking out in attack. Tia saw another fox hanging onto the bird's tail.

She ran to help. Her boots sank into the boggy ground and she struggled to pull her feet free.

'Help me!' the swan called again. The fox in front of her caught her neck and bit down. The swan flung it off but the other fox dragged harder at her tail.

Tia pulled her sling and two pebbles from her pocket. She quickly hurled one after the other. Both found their mark and the foxes leaped into the air.

'Leave that bird alone!' Tia shouted. With a heave she tore her feet free and squelched towards the foxes, her sling humming.

'I warned you!' She let fly and both foxes ran, the stone bouncing after them.

Stuffing the sling away, Tia hurried to the swan. Her neck was bleeding and her tail was chewed and battered. She shuffled protectively over her nest and hissed at Tia.

'I won't hurt you,' Tia said.

'How can you understand me?' the swan asked.

Tia automatically touched the familiar space on her shirt but the bump of the emerald wasn't there. Of course, she'd given it to Finn. She'd forgotten in all the excitement. 'I don't know,' she said truthfully. 'I want to help.'

'Find Orn,' the swan said.

'Who's Orn? Where is he?'

'He's the Swan Keeper of Holmurholt. He went that way.' The swan pointed unsteadily with her beak. 'He's checking our nests.'

'I'll go as fast as I can,' Tia promised.

After a few steps she found herself on firmer ground and began to run. Halfway round the island she caught sight of a tall, skinny man.

'Orn!' Tia yelled, running faster and flailing her arms to attract his attention. 'A swan's been attacked by foxes. I think they were trying to get her eggs,' she panted.

'Show me,' Orn said urgently.

Tia led the way back to the swan. Another had joined her. 'It's her mate,' Orn said.

'We've come to help,' Tia told the agitated birds. She turned to Orn. 'What are you going to do?'

'I'll take her to the Lady Ondine. She'll use her magic pearl to heal the swan.'

Tia's heart began to race. Perhaps she'd be able to see the High Witch and her pearl more quickly than she'd hoped.

'Will it be all right if I come with you – to see the High Witch heal the swan?' Tia asked.

Orn's face broke into a beaming smile. 'Of course,' he said heartily. Tia thought he sounded a bit relieved.

As the Swan Keeper carefully wrapped the injured bird in his coat and lifted her up, the other swan settled on the nest. Orn strode off towards a boat beached in the reeds and placed the swan in the stern. He and Tia pushed the boat out. She scrambled in and the Swan Keeper took the oars. As he pulled away Tia realised that there was no bridge connecting the main island to the others. The only way onto it was by boat.

As Orn rowed steadily, Tia trailed her hand in the water and tried to work out why she was still able to talk to animals. Orn said, 'Tell me about yourself. Are you a Trader? You're fairer than most.'

Tia told him her invented story of being lost as a baby and taken in by Traders who brought her up as their own. The Swan Keeper listened carefully and asked her questions. Tia had to think quickly, making sure her made-up facts matched the rest of her story. She was relieved when the boat bumped into a small jetty and Orn lost interest in her tale.

'Here we are.' Orn moored the boat and lifted out the swan. 'This way.'

Tia took a deep breath and walked beside Orn to the palace. Soon she would see her mother again, for the first time in eight years.

Chapter Three

Ondine

Orn and Tia hurried along a stone-flagged path winding through grass dotted with drifting white feathers. Swans grazed the grass, making tearing noises as they pulled at it with their beaks.

When they reached the palace the Swan Keeper, with Tia close behind, strode up the stone steps and through the open door into a lofty hall.

'What do you think you're doing!' a voice boomed. A tall man in black, carrying an ebony cane topped with a silver swan, strode towards them.

'I've got an injured swan, Grimmar,' Orn said. 'You know how the Lady Ondine loves her swans – she'll want to heal it as soon as she can.'

Tia didn't believe that for a moment. None of the High Witches loved anything except riches and power.

'Very well,' the man in black said. 'Come with me.'

As Tia took a step forward Grimmar held her back with his cane.

'Who is this…' he sniffed '…disreputable creature?' He looked down his long nose at Tia.

'I'm not disreputable!' she protested.

'Indeed?' Grimmar looked Tia up and down from her tousled hair to her mud-caked boots.

'She found the swan and helped me with it,' Orn said, staring intently at Grimmar. 'She's a Trader child – she has a way with the birds.'

Grimmar's eyebrows rose. He lowered his cane. 'Very well.' He turned towards a flight of stairs spiralling dizzily upwards.

Tia scampered after the two men. Why had it made a difference when Orn said she was a Trader? There hadn't been any wanted notices with her picture on it in the town and no-one had taken any notice of her despite her Trader clothing. Perhaps it was nothing to do with being a Trader; perhaps Grimmar had been impressed by what Orn had said about her way with swans.

Still, she was careful to note the way they were going in case she had to make a quick escape. And she felt in her pocket for the reassuring touch of her sling and pebbles.

By the time they'd gone through wood-panelled corridors on the top floor and entered a spacious chamber, Tia was on her toes, all her senses alert for danger.

'You may place the bird on that table,' Grimmar said, pointing with his cane. 'I shall inform the Lady Ondine you are here.' He left, the sound of his cane tap-tapping down the corridor.

Orn lowered the swan onto a large table in the centre of the room, unwrapped his coat and folded it around the swan like a nest. 'She's not doing well.'

The bird's long neck drooped till her beak touched the table top.

'You'll be all right,' Tia reassured her. 'I'm sure the Lady...' She swallowed. It was hard to say her mother's name. '...Ondine will be able to help you.'

'She will,' Orn said. 'The High Witch treasures the swans.'

'Indeed I do,' a voice said.

Tia turned slowly, making herself as small as she could beside the rangy Swan Keeper.

And there was her mother.

Ondine stood in the doorway. Her hair, exactly the same red-gold shade as Tia's, was tied back and bound by a diadem. A lustrous pearl hung from the golden circlet and rested on Ondine's forehead. Her expression was full of concern as she looked from Orn to the swan. She didn't seem to notice Tia at all.

But you're my mother, Tia protested silently. *Don't you realize who I am?*

Feelings tumbled through Tia: longing for her mother to know her, yet fear she'd be recognised as the jewel thief; anger at her mother for betraying the dragons, yet yearning for Ondine to care about her.

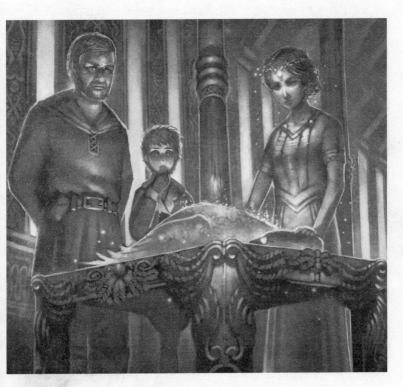

With the feelings clashing inside her, Tia watched Ondine examine the swan with gentle hands. The High Witch closed her eyes and the pearl on her forehead began to glow. Gradually the wounds on the bird's neck healed and her rump grew new, smooth feathers. She rose on steady feet, flapped her wings vigorously and honked.

Ondine opened her eyes and laughed. The sheen on the pearl faded.

'As you can see, the bird is healed, Master Orn,' she said to the Swan Keeper. 'Now, tell me, how did this happen?'

Orn explained about the foxes and Tia's part in driving them away. He pushed her forward. 'I brought the girl to you. I thought you'd want to see her.'

Tia stood with her head down.

'You did well, Master Orn,' Ondine said. 'I'll send a reward to your house. Now, take the swan back to her nest.'

Tia wondered if the reward was for bringing the swan – or bringing her. Still keeping her head down, she went to help the Swan Keeper.

'Wait, swan child.'

Tia's head flicked up. 'I'm not a swan child.' *I'm a DragonChild*, she thought defiantly. 'I'm Patia,' she said aloud, using yet another Trader name in case the High Witch had heard the names 'Nadya' and 'Sura' that she'd used before.

Ondine nodded, her expression solemn. 'How is it, Patia, that you have a Trader name yet look more like a Tulayan?'

Tia repeated her tale.

Ondine took Tia's face in her hands and murmured, 'You look so like me as a child.' She dropped her hands. 'I like you, Patia. You must stay with me. Come.'

The High Witch took Tia to a set of modest chambers. She pulled on a plaited rope and a tall girl, a few years older than Tia, appeared almost at once. She stared at Tia with round, surprised eyes as she bobbed a curtsey to the High Witch.

'Thora,' the witch said, 'this is Patia. She is to be my companion and you will be her maid. Find her suitable clothes and bring her to me in the white room tomorrow morning.'

With that, Ondine left. Tia glared at Thora. Why did people always want to change the way she dressed? 'I don't want fancy skirts. I want a tunic and trousers.'

Thora bobbed a curtsey. 'Whatever you wish.'

The girl's polite answer made Tia feel mean. 'What I'd really like is something to eat,' she said. It was almost evening and she was hungry. 'And please don't curtsey to me. I'm nobody special.'

'You're special to the Lady Ondine,' Thora said.

'I don't know why.' Perhaps, Tia thought, it was because the High Witch was on the lookout for a Trader child and, now she'd found one, meant to keep her close. Though that was dangerous, it suited Tia. She could find out all about the pearl, which would make it easier to steal.

Thora was worse than a limpet on a rock. She hung rich clothes in the cupboard in Tia's bedroom. She showed Tia the bathing room and when she'd finished her bath, there was Thora in the main chamber setting a table with food.

Thora pulled out a chair for her. Tia plumped down, wondering how she was ever going to get rid of the maid. 'I'm tired,' she said. 'I think I'll go to sleep after I've eaten.'

Thora bobbed one of her irritating curtseys, rushed into the bedchamber and turned down the covers.

She curtseyed again when she came back. 'I shall be sleeping in the outer room. Please call me if you need anything.'

'I won't,' Tia said. 'You don't have to stay with me.'

'It's what the Lady Ondine has instructed me to do.' Thora left the room and closed the door. Tia was sure she'd locked it. She tried the handle and the door opened.

Thora sat bolt upright on the small cot she'd been lying on. 'What can I do for you?' she asked.

Tia hadn't expected that. 'Um, what time does the Lady Ondine want to see me tomorrow?' It was the only thing she could think of, though she really wanted to ask why Thora wouldn't go away and leave her alone.

'She rises at dawn to study her magic. After that she has breakfast and then goes to the white room to do her sewing.'

Sewing! Tia couldn't imagine anything worse. She went back to her bedroom feeling like a prisoner. She was never going to be left alone to steal the pearl.

Chapter Four

The Pearl

Tia tossed and turned. Thoughts of Ondine raced around her head, mixed up with the few shadowy memories she had of her mother: a snatch of song, a warm hug, the sound of delighted laughter. How could these memories be true? Ondine was a cruel High Witch. She and her sisters only wanted to rule Tulay and become rich – that was why they'd stolen the dragons' jewels of power.

Tia turned her pillow over and pressed her hot cheek into its cool surface. How could her beloved father have married such a woman? And why hadn't her father kept his promise to find her and bring her home? Had Ondine done something terrible to him? After all, she had abandoned Tia to the dragons. She could have abandoned her husband too. Or done something even worse.

Tia sat up and hurled her pillow across the room. She hated Ondine. And now she was the High Witch's captive, with Thora acting like a jailer.

Tia needed fresh air. She got out of bed and stamped towards the open window, and a faint green glow caught the corner of her eye. Curious, she turned and found herself in front of a mirror. In the pale moonlight from the window Tia's face was only an indistinct blur but on her chest, just beneath her neck where the emerald had rested, was a small, hazy patch of luminous green.

Tia snapped a flame onto her finger and her image appeared clearly. But the green glow was gone. There was no sign of colour on her skin.

She clicked the light off and the green patch reappeared.

Thoughtfully Tia picked up her pillow and went back to bed. Four of the High Witches had worn the jewels in a gold or silver setting, only touching them to make use of their power. Skadi had set the sapphire in a bracelet designed to keep the jewel in contact with her skin, but she didn't wear it all the time. She took it off each night. Tia didn't know what Ondine did with the pearl.

Tia had worn the emerald continuously for many weeks. In all that time it had lain against her skin.

She must have absorbed some of its power. That was why she was still able to talk to animals and birds.

Tia snuggled down into the bed and smiled. She'd be able to talk to Loki after all. They could make plans with Finn.

She fell fast asleep until Thora shook her awake in the morning.

'Hurry, the Lady Ondine is waiting for you.'

After a quick breakfast Tia put on her new tunic and trousers while Thora hopped impatiently from foot to foot.

'Be quick. The High Witch is anxious to see you.'

Ondine was supervising work in a room overlooking the lake. Seamstresses, milliners and fan makers were seated under the windows, making use of the light. In the middle of the room was a long table. Quill makers sat at one end, trimming and cutting feathers to turn them into writing instruments. At the other end, plume makers assembled falls of feathers for helmets.

'Lady, I've brought Patia.' Thora bobbed. 'She slept in late – I had to wake her.'

'I expect she was very tired,' Ondine said. 'She's

been journeying for a long time in search of her parents.' She laid a hand on Tia's shoulder. 'I'm going to teach you a special skill. Thora, you may work with the seamstresses for now.'

Ondine guided Tia into another room. It was simply furnished with a table under a window and a chair on either side. Tia's heart sank when she saw what was on the table: a pile of fabric, a heap of tiny white feathers, needles and thread.

Sewing. Tia had never sewn anything in her life. She was sure she'd hate it. She was right.

First she learned how to stitch each minuscule feather onto a scrap of cloth. When she could do that without stabbing her fingers or breathing too hard and making the feathers fly away, Ondine showed her how to stitch them into neat rows.

Why can't I make plumes for helmets? Tia thought as she finished yet another fluffy row. *Or quills? That would be a bit more interesting.*

Ondine inspected Tia's work. 'Hmm. This is good enough for you to stitch a trimming.' She gave Tia a narrow band of cloth and told her to cover it in feathers.

Tia stitched resentfully for the whole morning. Outside the sun shone on the blue waters of the lake and the swans sailed by.

Ondine sewed away without speaking. Tia sneaked a glance at the pearl resting on her brow. She decided that the witch wouldn't wear the diadem while she slept: it would be too uncomfortable. If Tia could discover where it was kept at night, then she could work out how to steal the pearl.

Ondine began to hum softly. It was a sweet melody and despite herself, Tia found it soothing. She relaxed into her chair. Then she remembered. It was the melody that had haunted her dreams. The song her mother had sung to her as a tiny child.

Tia's needle slipped, stabbing into her finger. Blood dripped onto the swan's down.

Ondine leaned forward and took Tia's hand. 'Clumsy child.'

She closed her eyes and the pearl on her forehead glowed. Tia's small wound healed instantly and the pearl dimmed. Ondine opened her eyes.

'The trim is spoiled,' she said frowning at the red splashes on the white down.

Tia snatched her hand away. 'I'll do it again.'

Ondine shook her head. 'You'll be more use collecting the swan's down I need.'

'Thank you!' Tia said, clasping her hands together in gratitude.

Ondine threw back her head and laughed. 'You are a creature of the wilds,' she said. 'You belong outside. Come.'

Tia was so relieved she almost fell over her own feet in her eagerness to escape the sewing room.

Chapter Five

Storm

Ondine ordered Grimmar to summon the Swan Keeper. While she was waiting for him she took Tia to the dining room. As they ate Ondine questioned Tia about her life with the Traders. Once or twice Tia almost tripped up and contradicted herself. She was relieved when the meal was over and Grimmar arrived with Orn.

Ondine spent some time talking to the two men. They kept glancing over at Tia then turning back and nodding to Ondine. Tia wondered what the High Witch was telling them.

At last Ondine left with Grimmar, and Orn came up to Tia.

'The Lady Ondine wishes me to instruct you in the ways of swan-keeping. You are also to collect down to replace the feathers you spoiled.'

Tia thought that didn't sound too bad – and certainly better than sewing fiddly little feathers onto slippery fabric.

Swan-keeping *was* hard but Tia loved it. Three times a day she helped Orn and his assistants feed the birds. They filled buckets with grain from the barrows they trundled out to the lake and used a scoop to hurl it onto the water. Some food sank and the swans dived for it. Most floated and the swans picked it off the surface with clattering bills.

Tia was astonished to see sneaky little coots walking their great big feet over the swans' backs to get at floating grain. She grinned as she listened to them chittering to themselves: 'This is good! Ooh, there's more over there! Move closer, swan...' The dignified swans just ignored their small friends.

While the birds on the lake were busy feeding, Orn, Tia and the other assistants took grass, weeds and cress to the nesting swans. Orn wrote down how many eggs there were in each nest and the day on which they were laid.

Although Tia worked non-stop Orn never let her out of his sight.

After several days, Orn told her to gather feathers for Ondine. 'The little ones,' he said. Tia pulled a face. This was the part of her work she disliked. Tiny feathers were difficult to collect. Wind scattered them quickly and water snatched them out of reach.

Grumpily, she ran after a ball of down bowling along the edge of the lake. She pounced and the elusive puff of feathers blew away over the grass.

The familiar dark shape of a jackdaw zoomed over her head, swooped on the down, picked it up and flapped back to Tia. It was Loki.

Tia bent down and the jackdaw pushed the swansdown into her hand.

'Thank you. That should help keep the High Witch happy – for today at least.'

Loki hopped back in alarm. 'You're speaking to me! You can't. You haven't got the emerald – have you?'

Tia laughed at Loki's confusion. 'No, I haven't got it.' While she pretended to search the ground for more feathers, she explained about the emerald and all that had happened to her since she arrived in Holmurholt.

'I've written it down for Finn.'

'I thought you might,' Loki said.

Tia glanced round. Orn was busy with his tally of new eggs. She wriggled into a thick patch of reeds. 'Quick, before Orn notices I'm missing,' she hissed.

She quickly took the note she'd prepared and tied it to the jackdaw's leg.

'I'm tired of being a messenger,' he grumbled.

'Never mind, when I've got the pearl I can take all the jewels back to the DragonQueen and everything will go back to normal.'

Tia wondered if that was true. The dragons wouldn't need her as a hostage once she'd returned the jewels of power to the DragonQueen. Where would she go? What would she do? Would Freya, her DragonMother, let her stay?

A cry rang out: 'Patia!'

'It's Orn. I have to go.' Tia wriggled backwards out of the reeds. Loki flew off, buffeted by a flurry of wind.

Tia waved her bag of feathers at Orn. 'It's full,' she shouted.

The Swan Keeper loped over to Tia. 'Don't disappear like that!' he said. His face was white. 'The Lady Ondine would be angry if I lost you or you came to harm.'

'Why?' Tia asked.

'Because…' Orn's face went red. 'That's none of your business, little Trader girl.'

A powerful gust of cold wind blew by, making Tia shiver and threatening to snatch away her bag of feathers. She clutched it to her. She wasn't going to spend the rest of the day chasing after more feathers no matter what the High Witch wanted.

Orn watched gathering clouds scud across the sky. 'There's going to be a storm. We need to check that the cygnets are penned in.'

Tia glanced at the darkening sky. There was definitely going to be a storm. *It's a pity I don't have the topaz,* she thought. *I could change the weather and make it safe.* But that was impossible. The best she could do was help make sure the orphaned cygnets were safe in their secure pens.

The storm raged all night.

Wind howled and shrieked outside Tia's room and rain thrashed against the window panes. It was hard to sleep until the noise died away in the early morning.

When she looked out of her window the next day Tia caught her breath. Houses had gaping holes in their roofs. Fences lay broken, trees were torn up by the roots and debris was scattered everywhere. People were trying to round up stock that had escaped from broken pens. Others were attempting to clear up the mess or sat hopelessly among the wreckage of their homes.

Thora came bursting in, dressed in sturdy work clothes and stout boots. 'Hurry. The Lady Ondine wants everyone to help.'

As soon as Tia had jumped into her old Trader clothes Thora grabbed her by the arm and rushed her down to the palace kitchen. It was abuzz with purposeful activity as soldiers gave work gangs instructions on where they'd be most useful.

'But what about the other islands?' a man asked. 'I've got brothers and sisters there.'

'You don't need to worry about them,' a soldier said. 'Their houses are stone built – they've not taken much damage. It's our island that got hit the worst.'

'Here.' Thora thrust a flask and packet of food into Tia's hand. She grabbed the same for herself. 'The Lady Ondine wants you to work with her.'

'Why?'

'I don't know. You can ask her yourself,' Thora snapped as they set off out of the palace.

Tia didn't reply. She was sure Thora was bad-tempered because she was worried about the damage the storm had done to the island.

Chapter Six

Mending and Unmending

Tia had guessed right. Thora sped through the shattered houses outside the palace and stopped at the most devastated one of all. A man and a woman were sitting on a heap of wood that had once been the walls of their house. They clutched each other tightly. Thora scrambled towards them over broken furniture and crockery. There was even a carved wooden horse, its legs missing and one ear hanging by a splinter.

'Mama! Papa!' Thora cried and threw her arms round her parents.

The three of them clung together.

'It'll be all right,' Thora cried, wiping the tears from her mother's face. 'The Lady Ondine will help us.' She hugged her parents. 'I'll be back as soon as I can.'

'I'm sorry,' Tia said to Thora and wished more than ever that she could have used the topaz to stop the storm.

Thora ignored her. They hurried on past broken houses and silent, shocked people to a place where the houses seemed untouched by the storm.

'How did these houses escape?' Tia asked.

'They didn't.' Thora pointed. 'Look.'

The High Witch stood next to a house with a gaping hole in its roof. Grimmar was by her side together with a group of servants and guards,

Ondine had her eyes closed and her hands raised towards the house. The pearl glowed on her brow. Tia watched in wonder as the broken beams grew whole again, sprang from the ground and settled into place. The reed thatch rose in a cloud over the house and rewove itself, plaiting a braid neatly along the ridgepole. When it was done, Ondine lowered her arms, opened her eyes and the pearl dimmed.

Thora approached her, bobbed a quick curtsy and gabbled, 'Lady, please, please help my parents, their house is destroyed.'

'I will come to your parents by and by,' Ondine said.

Thora pleaded, 'But Lady...'

'Enough.' Ondine beckoned to Tia. 'Patia, attend me.'

Tia groaned inside. It was bad enough that she had become the High Witch's favourite but now she had to follow her while Thora could do nothing but wait for help. The look on the maid's face and her bunched fists told Tia that Thora resented that deeply.

She wasn't the only angry person. Though Ondine whisked from place to place restoring houses and farms, some of those who waited glowered behind her back, muttering as she helped their neighbours first. Tia glared at a family who sat by their wrecked farmhouse mumbling that the witch should hurry up and help them.

They're not hurt, she thought, *why don't they start helping themselves?* At least Thora had begun rescuing her parents' belongings, while her mother sat silently hugging the wooden horse and her father hauled debris into separate piles.

Ondine reached Thora's house last. It took her some time to put the house and its contents back together. When she had done, Thora's mother silently held out the wooden horse. Ondine mended it. The woman snatched it back, clutched it to her chest and rocked back and forth.

Ondine put a gentle hand on the woman's head. As the pearl glowed the woman stopped rocking and her glazed eyes cleared. Her broken mind mended, she jumped up. 'Oh my!' she said, taking in the restored house. 'Thank you, Lady.' She curtseyed deeply.

Thora bobbed her thank-you and her father bowed.

'Are you returning to the palace now, Lady Ondine?' Thora asked.

'No, we still have work to do.' She gestured to Tia and set off towards the edge of the lake.

Orn and his staff had been hard at work helping to rebuild the swans' nests. The birds were busy too, moving material with their bills, gathering it under their tails and building new nests on the site of their old ones.

Ondine helped speed the nest-building but even she couldn't heal the smashed eggs.

Orn's expression was glum. Tentatively Tia said, 'The Lady Ondine has worked hard to mend what she can.'

'What she mends, she can un-mend. What she heals, she can un-heal,' Orn muttered.

'Is that true?' Tia asked.

Orn shrugged. 'So they say.'

Tia remembered how the people of Askarlend had reacted when they saw her use the ruby to defeat High Witch Skadi. They had been afraid of her. They'd thought she might turn on them and use the ruby against them.

I would never have done that, Tia thought. *But a High Witch would.*

Chapter Seven

The Book of Shadows

Her work done, Ondine returned to the palace. She told Grimmar to summon Thora.

'You,' she said Tia. 'Come with me.'

The witch's chambers were modest and simply furnished. She led Tia through the entrance hall and the living rooms and into a side corridor ending in a locked door. She turned the key and went in.

On the other side of the door was a magic laboratory lined with books. They ran from floor to ceiling except where a high, wide window overlooked the lake. Beneath the window was a long table covered with familiar-looking phials, dishes, glass tubes and bottles of magic ingredients. They resembled the ones Tia had seen in Drangur where the High Witch Malindra had practiced her evil magic.

Ondine's no different from her, Tia thought. It was only then she realised she'd begun to think Ondine might not be as bad as her sisters after all.

A huge book lay open on a stand in the middle of the table. In front of it was a white marble dish lined with swans' down. Ondine unfastened the diadem from her hair and laid it wearily in the dish. The creamy pearl glimmered in light from the window. Ondine stroked it with a reverent fingertip and smiled at it like a parent might smile at a child.

She really loves that pearl, Tia realised with a shock. She took a step nearer. Ondine spun round. 'Do not approach my pearl!' she commanded.

Tia stumbled back. 'I didn't mean any harm, Lady,' she said wondering why the witch had brought her here if she was so protective of the pearl.

Ondine encircled Tia's shoulder. 'Give me your hands,' she said.

Tia held them out and Ondine gripped them in her free hand.

With Tia pinioned, the witch took her a few steps closer to the table until she could see the pearl clearly. It cast a white sheen like glowing moonlight touched with the blue-grey shadows of a cloudy night. Tia longed to pick it up.

Ondine's hands gripped tighter. 'Can you read?'

Tia shook her head, although she could read perfectly well.

Ondine shook her head, mockingly. 'Oh dear. If you were able to, you would see what is written in my Book of Shadows here. Never mind, it doesn't matter.'

The witch seemed to lose interest. She pulled Tia away and closed the book.

They left the magic laboratory, Ondine carefully locking the door behind her, and went back to the living chambers. Ondine dropped the key onto a chest by her bed.

'I'm tired. Sit with me until Thora arrives.' Ondine lay on her bed and Tia perched on the end. 'Amuse me, tell me one of your Trader tales.'

Relief washed over Tia. She could easily do that; she'd had plenty of practice telling stories to the High Witch Yordis. She told the tale of Prince Kaspar and the Skrimsli bear. Ondine was laughing delightedly at Tia's funny voices and extravagant gestures when there was a knock on the door.

'Come in,' she called, still laughing.

Thora entered with her usual bob. Ondine waved her to a footstool. 'Finish the story then you may go,' she told Tia.

Tia wound up the tale as quickly as she could then slid off the bed and left the room.

Outside Ondine's chambers she sagged against the wall. Did the High Witch know she was the thief? If not, why else would Ondine have tempted her with a close sight of the pearl and watched her reaction so carefully? And Tia had read the runes written across the open page of the Book of Shadows. They said: To Catch a Thief.

Tia lay awake early the next morning, thoughts racing through her mind: should she try and steal the pearl now, or wait for a better opportunity? She hadn't planned to take it yet but the chance might not come again, not if Ondine suspected that Tia was the thief.

A faint flush of yellow light seeping through the window told Tia that sunrise was coming. If she was going to steal the pearl it had better be now. She dressed quickly, opened the door, and crept past Thora who was snoring loudly in the outer room.

Tia climbed to the top of the dizzying spiral staircase and sped through dim corridors to Ondine's chambers.

There weren't any guards at the witch's door. *She must feel very safe if she hasn't got guards*, Tia thought.

She opened the door a crack. Dawn light filtered into the room through closed shutters. It glinted on the laboratory key still lying where Ondine had dropped it on the chest beside her bed. She had her back to Tia.

Holding her breath, Tia crept forward. She picked up the key. Ondine stirred, turned over. Tia froze, expecting the witch's eyes to open and widen with anger at the sight of the thief. With a soft sigh Ondine settled again.

Tia relaxed. She made her way silently to the magic laboratory, turned the key in the lock and went inside.

The pearl shone pure and clear in its feathery nest. Tia leaned forward to see it better. Its soft radiance seeped into her. She felt as though she were glowing too. She reached for the pearl and found herself unable to move for rapture.

Tia wondered vaguely if she was dreaming – or perhaps floating underwater. She couldn't think clearly, her sight was blurred, her hearing muffled. And she didn't seem able to move. A figure she vaguely recognised wavered indistinctly in front of her. It spoke, the words seeming to come from very far away:

'This spell of mine I now negate
Return her to her rightful state.'

Immediately Tia was wide awake. It was full daylight. Ondine stood in front of her, with Thora beside her, smiling in triumph.

Chapter Eight

Dragon Spell

Tia had fallen into Ondine's trap. She'd been tempted into trying to steal the pearl before she was ready, and caught by Ondine's spell.

'Did you really think you could escape me, thief?' Ondine jeered.

Tia was stiff from standing in one position while she'd been ensnared by the spell. She moved awkwardly to pull herself upright. 'I'm not the thief,' she insisted. 'I only wanted to look at the pearl – it's so beautiful I couldn't help myself.'

'Liar!' Thora sprang forward, waving Tia's green book. She must have searched Tia's belongings. 'There are plans in here of Drangur and Kulafoss castles. And you've torn pages out – I bet they were plans too.'

Tia glared at Thora. 'How dare you go through my things!'

'I instructed her to,' Ondine said. 'All Tulay knows the jewel thief is a Trader girl. I told Thora to look for proof it was you. And she has found it.' The High Witch leaned forward. 'But there was no sign of the jewels. Where have you hidden them?'

Tia knew only too well how the jewels overpowered any human who handled them. She had been temped into using some of them and the results had been disastrous. Ondine couldn't hope to control all the jewels. Only dragons could do that.

Greed blazed in Ondine's eyes. The look on her face made even Thora step back.

Suddenly a hideous noise screeched through the palace. The glass in the window cracked in a zigzag from top to bottom. Ondine, Tia and Thora clapped their hands over their ears.

'The spell!' Ondine shouted above the tumult. 'The spell has caught a dragon!'

Tia flew to the window. High above the hills rose the great spell snake. It was holding something in its jaws. It shook its head from side to side, dropped the thing in its mouth and plunged after it. The dreadful shrieking died away into a throbbing hiss.

Fear gripped Tia as tightly as the spell had gripped the thing its mouth. Finn – the spell snake must have caught Finn!

Ondine stared at Tia's stricken face. 'You are in league with a dragon!'

Tia couldn't speak – all she could think of was Finn in the jaws of the snake spell. Ondine seized Tia's arm. 'And the dragon has the jewels, hasn't it?'

Tia still couldn't speak. She shook her head.

'Pah!' Ondine shoved Tia towards Thora.

'I'll deal with you later,' she hissed at Tia. 'First I have a dragon to attend to and the jewels to claim.'

She rushed out, slamming the door behind her.

Tia hung her head. Why hadn't she confessed to Finn she was a witch-child who could see the snake spell? Then he wouldn't have flown into it, even if he had despised her for being a witch. What could she do to help him now?

She clenched her fists. She couldn't do anything while she was a prisoner. Tia turned and ran. Thora flung herself in front of the door and spread her arms.

'No you don't!'

There was only one thing that would frighten Thora. Tia conjured up the biggest fireball she could. It sizzled in her palms, writhing with flame. She took aim. Thora screamed and ran for cover.

Tia doused the fireball, wrenched the door open and sped to the stairs. Three of Ondine's guards had reached the top. Tia didn't have time to make another fireball. She dodged between the guards and leapt onto the polished wooden stair rail. She didn't look down. She was afraid of heights and knew if she so much as glimpsed the floor far below she'd lose her grip and fall. She kicked at the rail and began to slide. Faster and faster she went, spiralling downwards. She whizzed past Grimmar on his way up. 'Stop!' he boomed.

She couldn't have, even if she'd wanted to: she was going too fast. She reached the bottom, shot off the end of the rail and hurtled into a servant. They tumbled onto a thick rug and rolled over like ninepins.

Grimmar was racing down the stairs. 'She's a thief – don't let her go!' he bellowed.

Tia shot to her feet and pelted out of the door, down the steps and along the road to the lake's edge. Startled swans honked in alarm, puffing themselves up and beating their wings.

'Sorry!' Tia called as she careered on.

She reached the jetty and jumped into one of the small boats tied to it. She fumbled with the knot. It wouldn't come loose.

Tia heard the pounding of feet and shouting. Grimmar's voice rose above the tumult. 'Catch her!'

The clumsy knot slipped free as Grimmar bounded onto the jetty. Desperately Tia grabbed

an oar, braced it against the jetty and pushed. The
boat spun out sideways and she dropped the oar into
the water. Grimmar knelt and reached for her. She
snatched the second oar. She thrust it at him, over-
balanced and stumbled backwards into the stern.
The oar flew from her grip and joined the other one
in the lake.

Tia scrambled into a sitting position and gripped
the sides of the boat. More people were joining
Grimmar on the jetty and it thundered and swayed
as they ran towards her.

'Give up.' Grimmar grasped the painter and pulled

the boat closer. 'There's no-one to help you now.'

All at once the air was full of swans. They honked and dived, wings thrumming. A flock of them landed on the jetty, puffed themselves up and charged towards the men, wings and necks out-stretched. Half the men jumped in the water to get away, the other half ran back up the jetty. Neither group escaped. The men on land faced more swans charging towards them. The men in the water found themselves surrounded by a flotilla of furious birds.

Two swans glided towards Tia's boat.

'Why are the men attacking you?' one honked. Tia recognised the swan she had rescued.

'I'm trying to get to my friend in the hills. He needs help. The men want to stop me.'

The swan clacked her beak angrily. 'You saved me from the foxes - we will save you from the men.'

The two birds pushed the oars back to Tia and escorted the boat as she rowed across the lake to the bank and jumped out.

The swans rose in the water, flapped their wings and honked in salute. 'Goodbye and good fortune. May you find your friend.'

As she ran towards the hills, Tia hoped against hope it wasn't too late to help Finn. She would never forgive Ondine for this.

Chapter Nine

Healing and Mending

Tia ran from island to island and on into the lower slopes of the hills. She dropped to her knees on the grass, exhausted.

I'm not going to reach him in time, she thought.

And if you did, what could you do to help? a mocking little voice said in her mind.

Tia ignored it. She'd defeated five High Witches already. She'd find a way to get the better of this one too. But she had to reach Finn before Ondine killed him. She got to her feet and forced herself to jog steadily up into the hills.

A fast drumming sound ahead caught her by surprise. A riderless horse, bridled and saddled, came galloping down the hill and flew past her, its nostrils flaring in fear.

'Tia!'

Loki barrelled out of the sky and flapped round her head. 'You've got to hurry. That witch has almost reached Finn. She'd be there already if her horse hadn't been afraid of the smell of dragon and thrown her.'

'I'm going as fast as I can,' Tia protested.

She felt as if a stone had lodged in her chest. What if she was already too late to save her DragonBrother?

'Hasn't the witch brought anyone with her?' she panted.

'Hah! She brought two soldiers. Their horses ran off in different directions as soon as they got a whiff of Finn.'

Tia nodded. She'd found her second wind and wasn't going to waste it on speaking. She kept going steadily until Loki said, 'Finn's on the other side of this hill. He fell by some trees.'

Tia dropped onto her stomach, elbowed herself to the top of the hill and looked over. Finn lay stretched out under the trees. His eyes were glazed and dull. His skin was a strange yellowy green instead of its natural copper. Smoke trickled weakly from his nostrils.

'Oh no,' Tia whispered. Ondine was leaning over the little dragon, her arms outstretched. Her eyes were closed and the pearl on her brow gleamed.

'Is she doing a spell?' Loki asked.

'Yes, a healing spell with the pearl.' Tia's breath caught in her throat. She'd expected Ondine to kill Finn. Hope, like a small bird, fluttered inside Tia. Perhaps Ondine felt pity for the little dragon? Maybe she wasn't completely wicked after all.

Loki's beady eyes fixed suspiciously on the witch. 'I thought she hated dragons?'

'She does.' Tia began to crawl over the hilltop.

'Wait!' Loki hopped in front of her. 'You can't fight the witch – she's a lot stronger than you. Throw yourself on her mercy and tell her that you're her daughter. It's your only hope – you have to do it.'

Tia wanted to believe what Loki said but she didn't dare. Silently she wriggled down the hill until she was as close to Finn and Ondine as she could be without revealing herself. She crouched in the thin undergrowth around the trees and spied through the leaves.

Ondine was concentrating hard but the pearl only shimmered palely. Finn drew a rasping breath, coughed and opened his eyes.

Ondine dropped her hands and the pearl instantly dimmed.

Finn lifted his head. Tia drew in a sharp breath. The pouch wasn't round his neck.

'Where are the jewels of power, dragon?' the High Witch demanded.

'I don't know what you mean about jewels.' Finn's head dropped back onto the grass.

Fury brighter than a fireball burned away Tia's hopes. Ondine wasn't showing pity for Finn. She'd healed him just enough to talk, but not enough to fight or fly away.

'Do something' Loki demanded.

Tia's mind worked furiously. 'Give me a minute – I'm thinking.' She was too full of anger and crushing disappointment to think clearly.

Loki cocked his head to one side. 'I'll help you.' The jackdaw squawked, flapped his wings noisily and fluttered up and down.

'Stop it, she'll see me!' Tia hissed.

Loki screeched louder and started to peck at Tia. She held her arms over her head to protect herself and stumbled to her feet.

'You!' Ondine glared unbelievingly at Tia.

Loki flew into the trees, still racketing.

Ondine made hauling movements with her hands. Tia felt herself being reeled in like a fish. As she was dragged along the grass she vowed she would never to do what Loki wanted and tell Ondine that she was her daughter.

Instead she pleaded, 'Please, Lady, don't hurt the dragon. He's done no harm.'

'Dragons always do harm. It's their nature,' Ondine said. 'As for you, I don't know how you managed to escape but since you did, I'll make use of you. Tell me where the jewels are and I'll spare this creature you seem so fond of.'

'I don't know,' Tia said. 'I really don't.'

Ondine tutted. 'Oh dear, I seem to have only one choice left.' She stared down at Finn. 'Tell me where you've hidden the jewels or I'll kill this child.'

She thrust out her arm and a lightning bolt appeared in her fist. The bolt sizzled, making Tia's hair crackle and stand on end.

'No.' With an enormous effort Finn raised his head again. 'You can't do it, you mustn't. She's your daughter.'

'My precious child was killed by dragons! By your kind!' Ondine shrieked. 'How dare you speak of her?' She raised the lightning like a spear and aimed at Finn.

'Don't!' Tia flung herself at Ondine. 'I *am* your daughter Tia. The dragons took me when the necklace was stolen. They cared for me. They were going to return me when the witches gave the jewels back.'

Ondine's face flickered with hope, despair, disbelief, anger. She lowered her arm. 'Prove it.'

Tia reached for her locket. But that, like the emerald, was gone.

'I thought so.' The lightning appeared in Ondine's hand again.

A soft thud near Tia's feet made her look down. Her locket and chain lay in the grass.

'Wait!' She scooped up the locket, clicked it open. She pulled off the scrap of paper covering Ondine's face and turned the locket to her mother. 'See, you and Papa gave me this when I was little. Do you remember?'

The bolt fizzled out. White-faced, Ondine took the locket. She looked from Tia to the pictures and back again. 'Oh, my child, what have I done?'

Tia ran into her mother's embrace.

As they held each other tightly, the pearl on Ondine's forehead glowed, pure as moonlight. It didn't fade until the hurt that Tia and her mother had carried for eight years was healed at last, and the broken bond between them was mended.

Chapter Ten

The Trickery of the High Witches

Ondine gave the locket back to Tia. 'Where did it come from? It just dropped from the sky.'

Tia thought she knew but she had more important things to deal with. 'I'll tell you later, Mama,' she said hurriedly, fastening the chain round her neck. 'First, please heal Finn. He's my DragonBrother.'

Ondine gave Tia's hand a gentle squeeze. 'Of course.'

This time Ondine didn't stop until Finn was fully restored, his skin back to its healthy coppery sheen.

Ondine opened her eyes and Finn promptly disappeared. 'Where is he?' Ondine said, bewildered.

Tia was surprised her mother couldn't see the little dragon, since Ondine was such a powerful witch.

'He's still there,' Tia said. 'He's disguised himself so the spell can't see him and hurt him again.' She glared at Finn. 'He didn't realise that your spell was especially powerful.'

Ondine glanced up at the shadowy snake still slithering around the hilltops. 'The attack on Finn weakened it. If he's careful, he'll be quite safe.'

She sat on the grass and patted a place next to her. 'Come, tell me all that's happened to you.'

Tia told Ondine about being kidnapped, about her life with Freya, Finn and the other dragons, and about her quest to recover their jewels so that she could prove she was a true DragonChild.

'My sisters are powerful and wicked,' Ondine said. 'You must be very wily and brave.'

Tia couldn't believe her ears. Ondine was criticising her sisters. 'But Mama, if they are so wicked why did you help them steal the necklace?'

'They tricked me,' Ondine said. 'I travelled to the Eldkeiler Mountains with a swansdown coverlet for the DragonQueen's new eggs. I had agreed to meet my sisters there. We approached the DragonQueen, each of us with a gift. She'd put the necklace round the nest. As we drew near, Malindra pushed me. I put out a hand to break my fall and touched the pearl. Immediately each of my sisters grasped a jewel.

They chanted a spell and I found myself transported with them here to Holmurholt.

'My sisters worked together to shrink the necklace. They divided the jewels between them and offered the pearl to me.' Ondine shook her head. 'I wouldn't take it. But the next day they came and told me that the dragons had killed you and your papa in revenge for the theft. I vowed to be the dragons' enemy from that moment on. I gave all my love to the pearl.' Ondine stroked Tia's cheek. 'As though a jewel could take your place, or Elio's!'

Tia hugged her mother. 'I'm alive, Mama, and Papa will be too. I'm sure of it.'

'Perhaps,' Ondine said sadly. She gave herself a little shake and held Tia at arm's length. 'Now, beloved child, you said that the dragons would send you home if the jewels were returned?' Tia nodded. 'Then, as you are already restored to me, the jewels should be re-set in the necklace and taken to the DragonQueen. My sisters threw the necklace away: they weren't interested in mere gold. But I thought it was beautiful and kept it.'

Finn sprang to his feet, his sharp dragon ears twitching. 'I can hear horses coming this way!'

'It will be my guards,' Ondine said. 'We'll go back to the palace with them and retrieve the necklace.'

'I should be with Finn,' Tia said, even though at that moment she wanted to stay with her mother more than anything.

'I understand,' Ondine said. 'I'll return as soon as I can.'

Two mounted guards, leading a riderless horse, rode up. The horses started to shy. The leading guard quickly dismounted and gave the horse's reins to his companion.

He ran to Ondine and dropped on one knee. 'You are safe, Lady! When the horses bolted we were afraid the dragon would overpower you.'

'Overpower me, the High Witch of Holmurholt!' Ondine said scornfully. 'As you can see, there is no dragon here.' Tia choked back a snort of laughter. 'It escaped,' Ondine went on. 'Your horses are afraid of the smell it left behind.'

Finn huffed. The horses pricked their ears and rolled their eyes.

The guard stood up. His eyes flickered to Tia. 'You caught the thief, Lady!'

'She's no thief,' Ondine said and to the guard's astonishment, the High Witch of Holmurholt embraced Tia.

The bemused guard escorted Ondine to her horse and locked his hands into a stirrup. She mounted, waved goodbye to Tia and galloped away with the guards.

Tia listened to the sound of hooves until all she could hear was wind in the leaves and a wedge of swans honking as they flew down to the lake.

'She's gone then?' a voice said overhead. Loki was perched on a branch above Tia's head. He held the pouch in one foot.

'Loki! I knew it was you who dropped the locket. How did you get the pouch?'

'I unpicked the cord round Finn's neck when the spell caught him. It was a good job I did. When you were talking to the witch I held the emerald and listened. I knew I was right – you had to convince her you're her daughter. That's why I dropped the locket.'

'Thank you, Loki.'

Loki shook his feathers. 'And I was listening just now. Trusting her is a mistake. She'll take one look at the jewels and want them all for herself. Then Tulay will be in worse trouble than ever. '

'But Loki...'

'I'm keeping them.' The jackdaw gripped the pouch and flew higher into the trees.

'Loki!' Tia called. It was no use. The bird and the jewels were gone.

Chapter Eleven

All the Jewels of Power

Tia and Finn went safely through the spell boundary to another copse of trees, this one with a stream winding through it.

'Loki won't give me the pouch,' Tia fretted. 'He said Mama wants to keep them for herself.'

Finn laughed. 'Loki always thinks the worst. Don't worry, DragonSister.'

Ondine rode back in the early afternoon with the necklace wrapped in a bundle of soft leather.

'You need the pearl to complete the necklace.' Ondine took off the diadem and put it in Tia's hands. 'This was never rightfully mine. The jewels were not intended for human use. You were right to get them back for the dragons – I'm proud of you.'

Tia gave the delicate circlet to Finn. He carefully unpicked the pearl with his claws, gave the jewel to Tia and held out the diadem to Ondine.

'I have no need of it now,' she said.

Finn flung it far away.

Ondine untied the bundle. Kneeling on the grass, she peeled back layers of cloth and revealed the necklace. Sunlight glinted on the intricately forged pattern of rose-gold. At one end was a chain, at the other, a link with a hooked clasp. In the front were six empty spaces.

'Now you can put the jewels in place,' Ondine said.

'No, I can't. I haven't got them,' Tia said.

'Who has?' Ondine asked, bewildered.

A familiar cawing made them both turn. Loki was perched on Finn's shoulder, the pouch in one foot.

'Him,' Tia said.

As she reached out for the pouch Loki hopped higher up Finn's shoulder. 'I still don't trust the witch.'

'I do, and so does Finn.'

'Are you and the bird talking to each other?' Ondine asked in surprise.

Tia explained about the emerald. 'But it's no use when he won't listen to me.' She glared at Loki.

Finn shot a burst of small flames over the jackdaw's head. He sprang into the air and dropped the pouch in his haste. Tia snatched it up.

'Don't blame me if *she* runs off with the jewels,' Loki mumbled. He settled back on Finn's shoulder, hunched up in a sulk.

Taking care not to be dazzled by the jewels' power, Tia placed each one in in its true setting: the emerald, the opal, the topaz, the sapphire, the ruby and the pearl. When the necklace was complete, the jewels flared with an unbearably intense light. Ondine and Tia threw their hands over their eyes; Finn and Loki thrust their heads under their wings.

The blaze died away. Tia squinted through her fingers at the necklace. She dropped her hands and stared in dismay.

'It's huge!'

The necklace had reverted to its proper size. It was much too large for Tia to handle.

'Only a dragon can carry it,' Finn agreed.

Tia sagged in disappointment. After all she'd done to steal back the jewels she wasn't going to be able to return them after all; Finn would have to do it.

'You'll just have to turn yourself into a dragon again,' Finn said.

'But…'

Finn held up a forefoot. 'This is your quest – you ought to finish it properly.'

Ondine smiled. 'Listen to your DragonBrother. You've earned the right to return the jewels.' She gave Tia a gentle push towards the opal.

Tia bent and touched it. She thought of being a dragon. Instantly, Dragon Tia appeared. She cracked her red-gold wings and spouted a stream of flames. In a burst of elation she sprang into the air, dipping and swooping through the sky.

The spell. She'd forgotten the spell. She curbed her wild excitement and spiralled cautiously back to earth.

She glanced around. 'I can't see the spell,' she said in surprise.

'Once the necklace was restored to its true form the spell died,' Ondine said. 'All the towns and their lands are free of it. The dragons rule Tulay once again, although they don't know it yet.'

Tentatively she reached out and touched Tia. 'You are a magnificent dragon,' she said, 'strong and wild. Your DragonMother will be proud of you, as I am.'

'All dragons are magnificent. That's our nature,' Finn said.

He sat on his haunches and helped fasten the necklace around Tia. He slotted the hook into the

first link of the chain to shorten it and draped the rest over her shoulder. It lay low down on her chest but she would be able to fly with it.

Tia snaked her head round and gently nudged Ondine. 'Will you ride to Drakelow?'

'Not yet. The dragons will have to know they can trust me first. Besides, I have to go back to Holmurholt. I am still a High Witch and I can use my magic to help people, even without the pearl. If they will let me.'

'It was the pearl they were afraid of, not you. They'll like you better without it,' Tia said.

'Perhaps. Now, let me see you fly away.'

'I'll come back to you, soon' Tia said.

Ondine took a few paces back. 'Goodbye – for now.'

Tia sprang into the air with Loki flying around her. Finn followed. Higher and higher the dragons went, beating their wings in the sky. They were on their way at last to return the necklace to its rightful owners, the mighty Dragons of Tulay.

Chapter Twelve

Return to Drakelow

As the snow-topped Drakelow Mountains rose before Tia she couldn't help thinking of the first time she'd been here. Then she'd been a small child stolen from its parents, clutched in the fist of a great red dragon, Andgrim, brother to the DragonKing. She'd been tired, cold and afraid. Now she was a dragon herself, afraid of nothing. Joyously she spiralled in the air, dived and sailed upwards again, revelling in the freedom of the sky.

A thunderous roaring made her backwing. A flight of dragons, led by Andgrim, was arrowing towards her and Finn. The formation split and gathered in a circle around Tia and her DragonBrother. They had no choice but to allow the Drakelow dragons to shepherd them to the plain at the foot of the mountains.

The whole flight landed in a flurry of churning dust.

Andgrim thundered towards Tia. 'Who are you? Why are you wearing the DragonQueen's necklace?'

He doesn't scare me, Tia thought. She drew herself up and said haughtily, 'I demand an audience with their majesties, the DragonQueen and DragonKing.'

'How dare you demand anything, you slip of a dragonet!' Andgrim roared, little flames licking his fangs.

'I dare because I have the jewels of power.' Tia gripped the topaz and thought of a storm. Thunder boomed, lightning cracked, hailstorms the size of boulders crashed around. Even the biggest of the dragons crouched under the onslaught.

Tia thought of sunshine and warmth. Instantly the storm was gone. The smashed hailstones turned to puddles and steamed in the sunshine.

She put her foot on the sapphire. Before Andgrim could blink she was behind him, on a ledge above his head.

'Where are you?' the red dragon bawled.

Tia sat on the ledge, regal as a monarch on her throne. 'Here. Now will you grant me an audience with their majesties?'

'Never!'

Andgrim drew a breath to hurl a stream of fire at Tia. She put her foot on the ruby. Strands of red light shot from it and enclosed Andgrim. He was frozen inside a time bubble. His astonished, angry face stared out as the bubble floated in front of Tia.

'Release him!' an imperious voice said.

The DragonQueen and her mate had flown in to see what the commotion was about. More dragons and dragonets landed behind them.

'Yes, majesty,' Tia said reverently. She kept one forefoot on the ruby and stabbed the bubble with a claw on her other. The bubble turned to red powder and Andgrim fell to the ground in an undignified heap.

Tia glided down to land in front of the royal dragons. Finn hurried to her side. They dipped their heads in a respectful greeting.

One of the dragonets nudged another. 'What's the copper freak doing with that gold dragon?'

It was Tia's old enemy, Torkil the bully. He was Finn's enemy too. Soon he was going to be very surprised indeed.

'Help me with the necklace,' Tia said to Finn.

Her DragonBrother carefully unhooked the chain and the necklace slid to the ground.

'I have taken back the jewels of power from the High Witches and now I return them to the DragonQueen.'

'Who are you?' the DragonKing asked.

A green dragon standing next to the queen spoke up: 'I know her.' It was Freya, Tia's DragonMother.

If the occasion hadn't been so solemn, Tia would have rushed up to Freya. She'd missed her dreadfully. Instead she stood proudly in front of the DragonQueen.

'Welcome home, beloved DragonDaughter,' Freya said formally. She turned to Finn, 'And to you, my dear DragonSon.'

'Didn't know he had a sister,' Torkil muttered. 'They're two freaks together – gold and bronze, huh.'

Andgrim had recovered his dignity well enough to cuff his son. 'Quiet!' he hissed.

'It's time for you to reveal yourself,' Freya said to Tia.

Tia stretched out her clawed forefoot for the last time and gripped the opal. She thought of herself as she really was.

A huge gasp went up as the golden dragon vanished and human Tia stood in her place.

'It's the witch-brat!' Torkil screeched. It earned him another cuff from his father.

The DragonKing scooped up the necklace and fastened it around the queen's neck. The dragons trumpeted their triumph till the sound threatened to dislodge the snow from the mountain tops.

When the tumult died away the DragonQueen beckoned to Tia. She stepped forward and the DragonQueen shielded her with a wing.

'Let no-one call Tia Freyasdaughter, a witch-brat. From henceforth she is to be known as Tia, the DragonChild.'

The mountains rang again with the exultant bellowing of dragons and Tia thought she would burst with pride. She was truly a DragonChild at last.

Tia, Finn and Loki sunned themselves on the rocks at Drakelow. The other dragonets lolled about too, watching the large dragons gathered in a meeting on the plain below.

'What do you think they'll decide to do about the High Witches?' Tia said. 'I mean, apart from Ondine. She's allowed to stay in Holmurholt because she helped me.'

'I heard that as soon as we go back to our keeps in the Eldkeiler Mountains, the witches are going to be banished. They're each being sent to an island off the coast. They're going to be forbidden to do magic,' Finn said.

He nudged Tia with his nose. 'Have you decided what you're going to do?'

'I've decided to go and stay with Mama for a while, so we can get to know each other. But I'm a DragonChild now. Mama will have to understand that even though I love her, I love my DragonMother too.' Tia sighed. 'It's hard dividing yourself between two mothers.'

'You're lucky,' a dragonet snarled. It was Torkil. 'Some of us don't even have one mother, thanks to your precious Ondine and her sisters.' The young dragon launched himself angrily from the rock and flapped away.

'What did he mean?' Tia asked Finn.

'His mother was killed in the war for the jewels,' Finn said.

Tia had known Torkil was motherless but not why. It would explain why he disliked her.

'I'm sorry about that, she said, 'but it wasn't Mama's fault. And she lost me and Papa. I wish I'd found him too, then Mama wouldn't be lonely when I'm not with her.'

Finn sent out dense swirls of smoke. 'And I wish I could find *my* father. Don't forget, he vanished during the war with the High Witches.'

The two friends looked at each other.

'Finding our fathers can be our next quest!' Tia said.

Loki cawed in protest. 'Haven't you had enough adventures?'

Tia and Finn didn't hear him. They were too busy making plans.

Deep in a cave in a faraway land, a sleeping man woke, as he had once in every year for eight years. Candles flickered all around him, bathing the cave in soft yellow light.

He sat up and wondered where he was. He rubbed his face and noticed a ring on his finger. It puzzled him until he remembered: *I have a wife, and I have a daughter*, he thought wonderingly. *A fearless little child who loves nothing better than to run barefoot through the woods.*

'I must go to them,' he said. He struggled to feet. What was that shape in front of him, blocking the way out of the cave?

With a jolt he realised it was a dragon. An enormous sleeping dragon.

A cold wind blew through the cave. The candles guttered and died. A profound cold seeped through the man's bones. He sank to the floor as his eyelids drooped, closed.

He began the ninth year of his slumbers.